At the Park

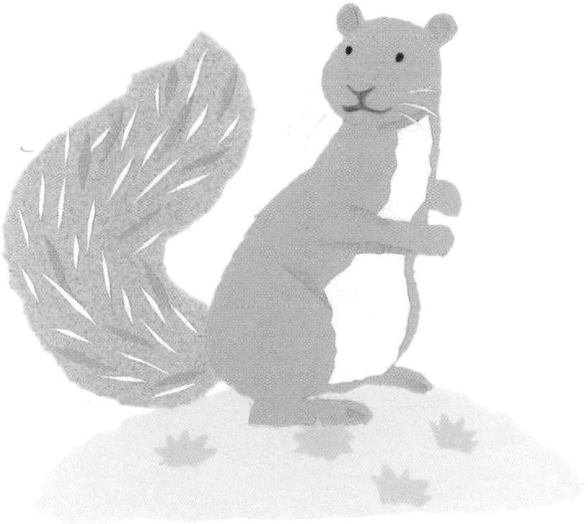

Maoliosa Kelly
Illustrated by Alex Ayliffe

RIGBY

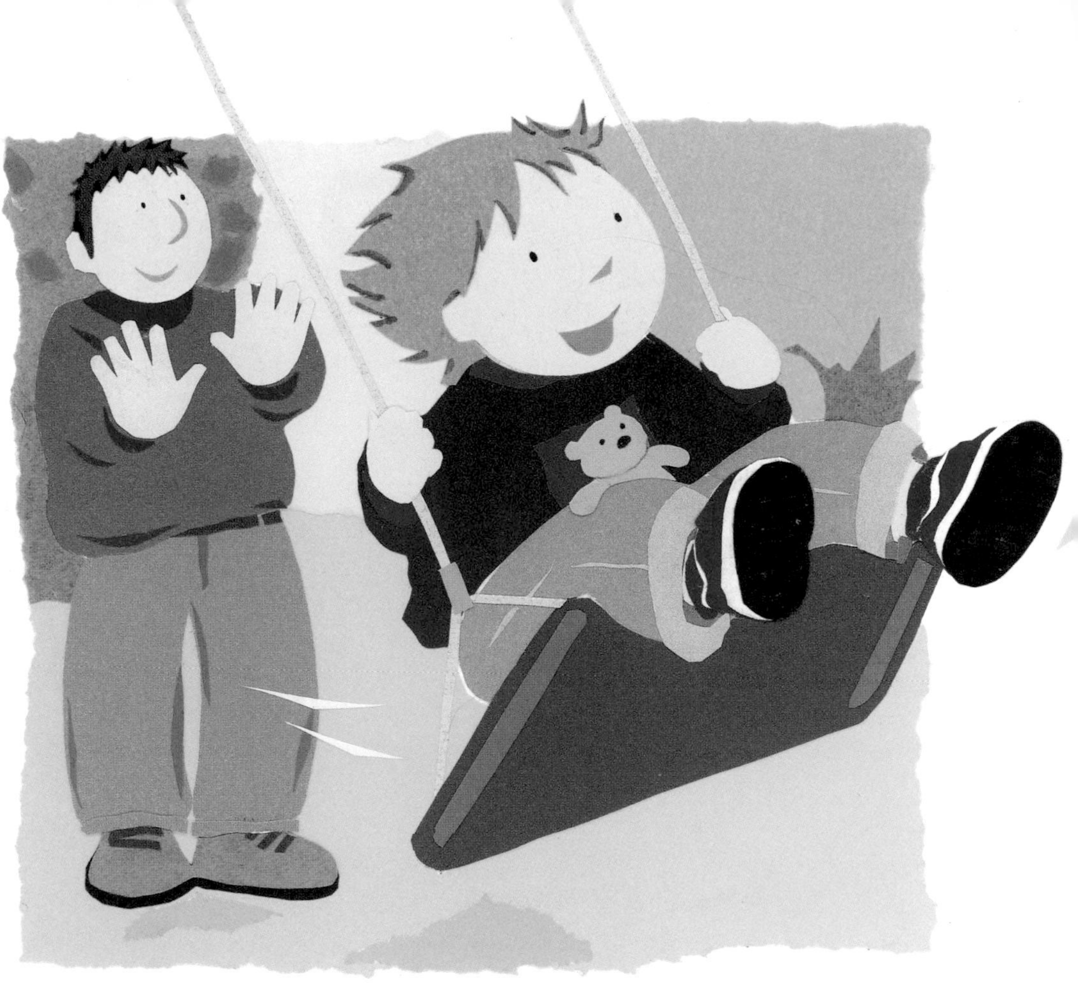

the swing

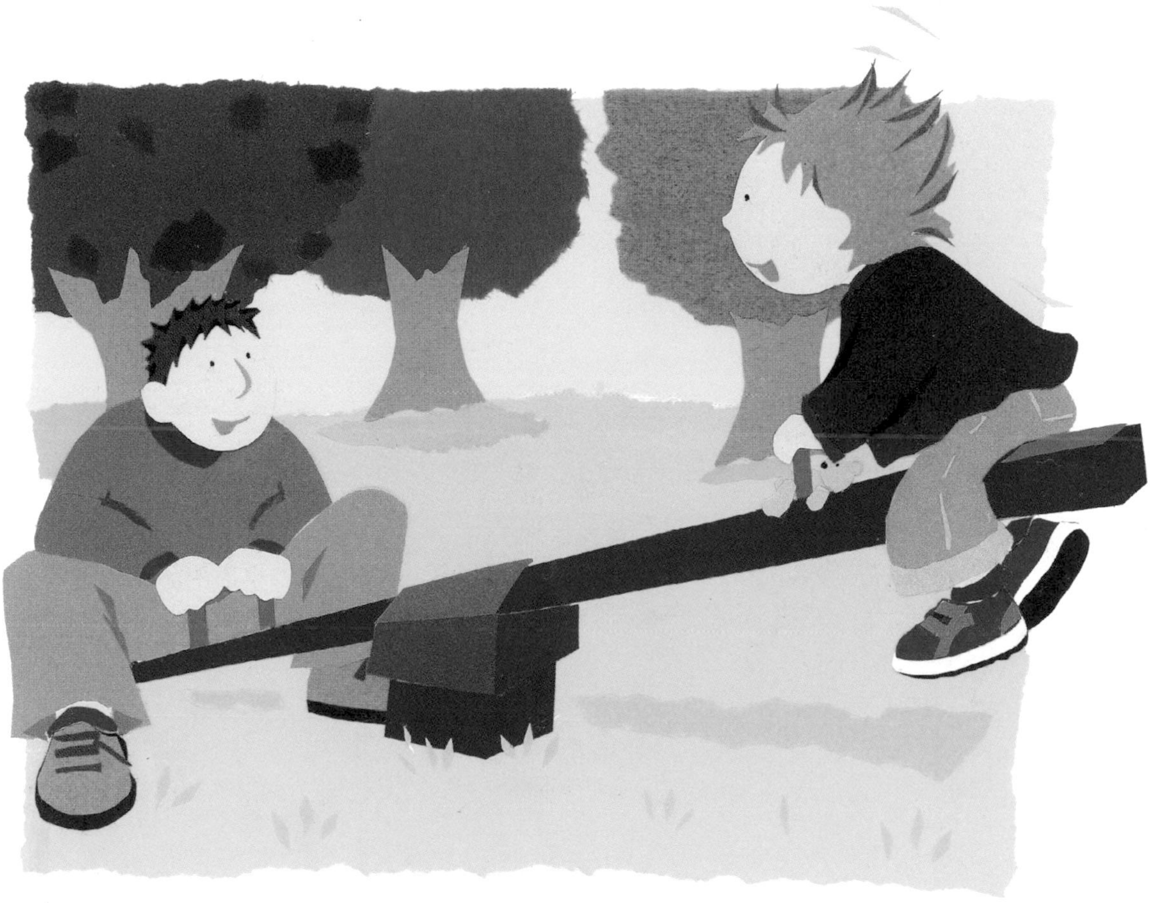

the see-saw

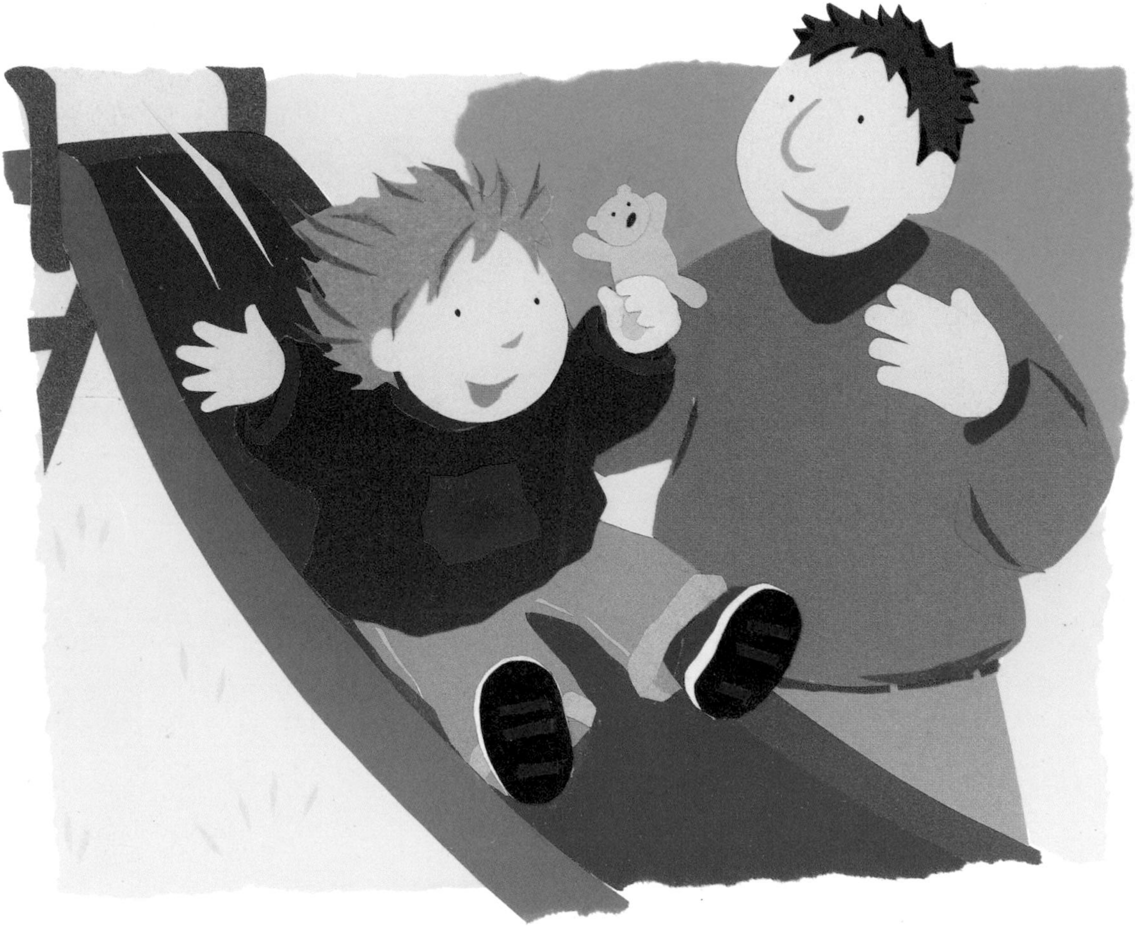

the slide

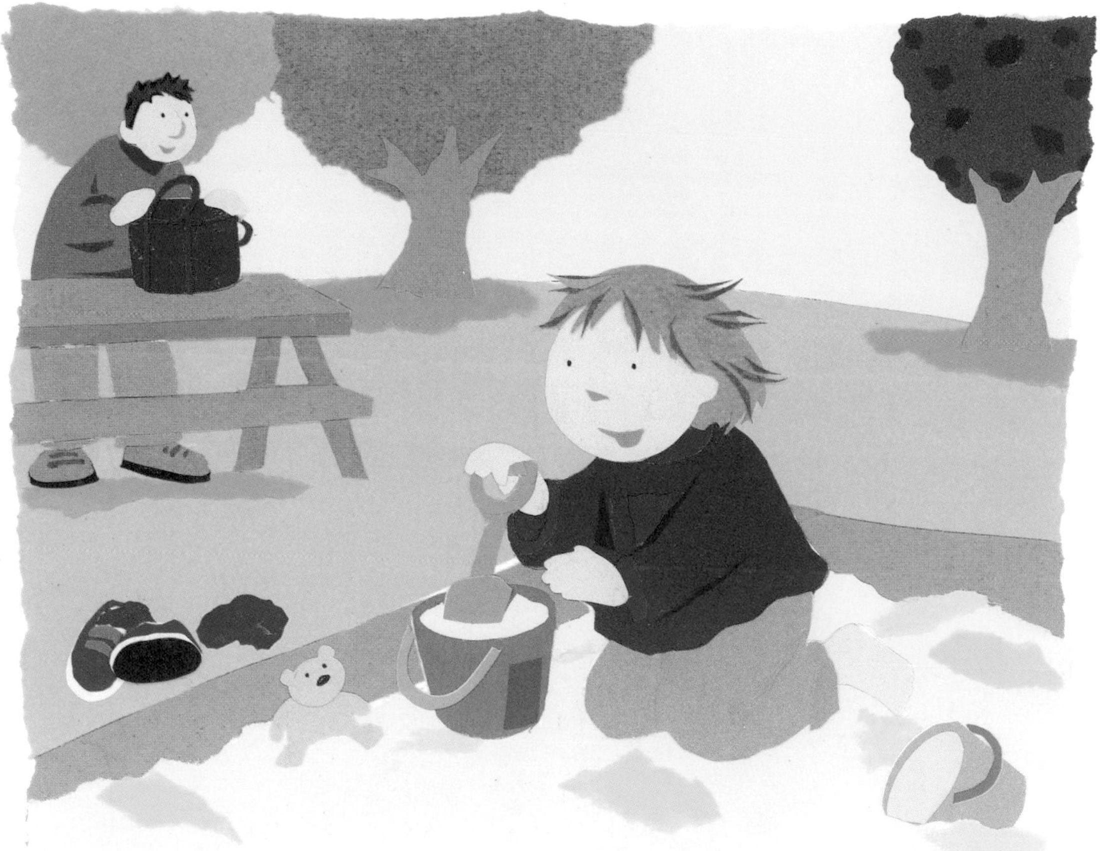

the sandpit

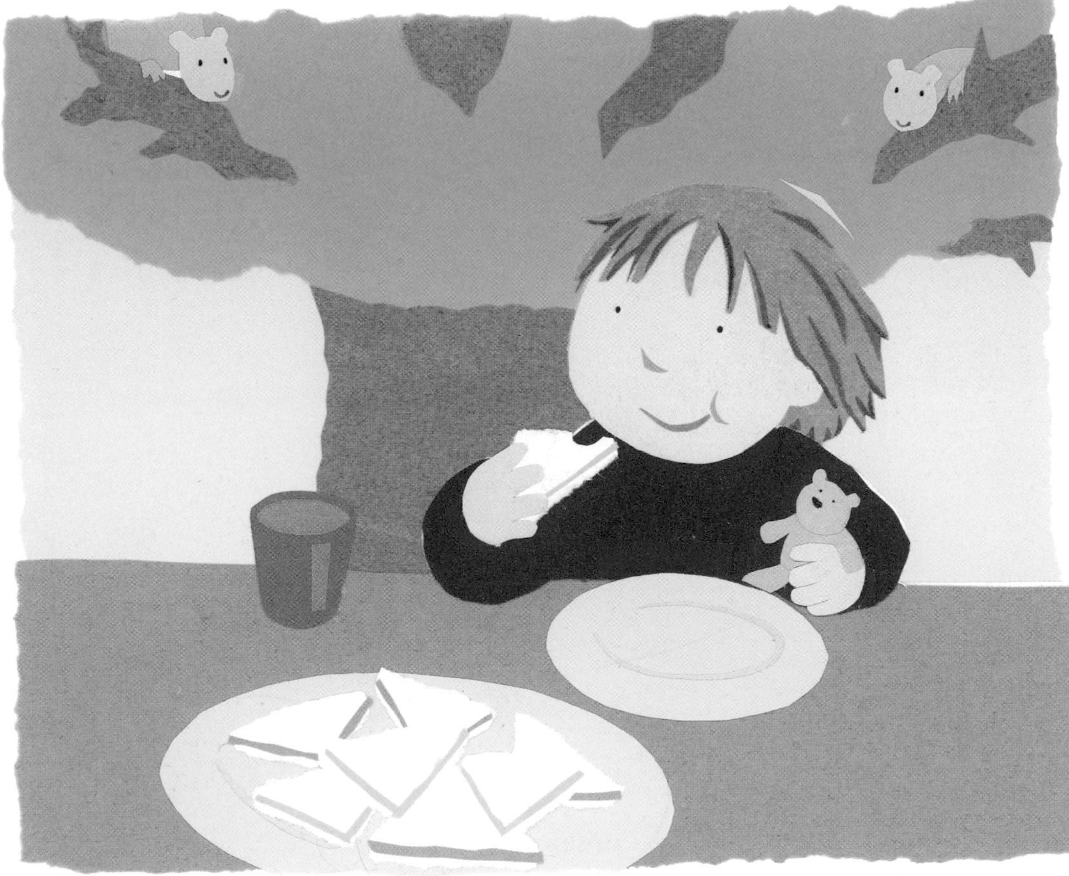

the sandwich

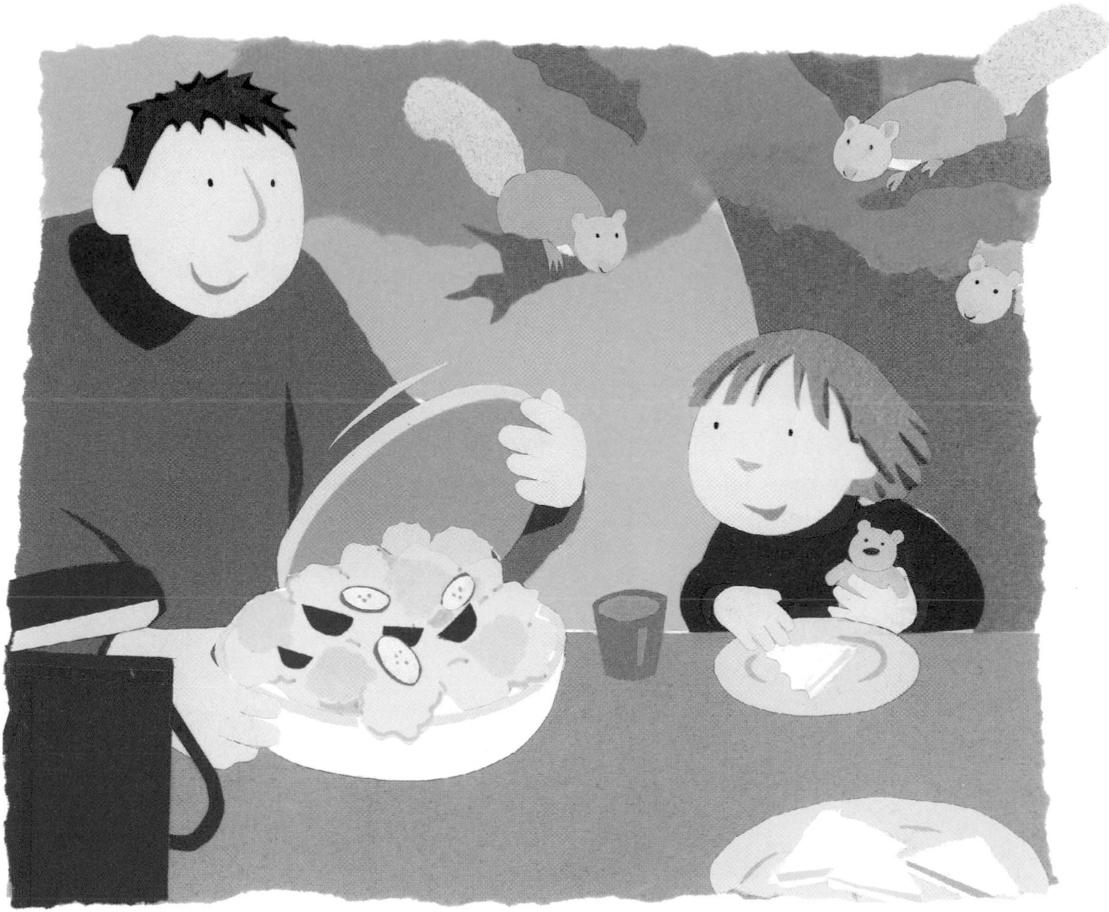

the salad

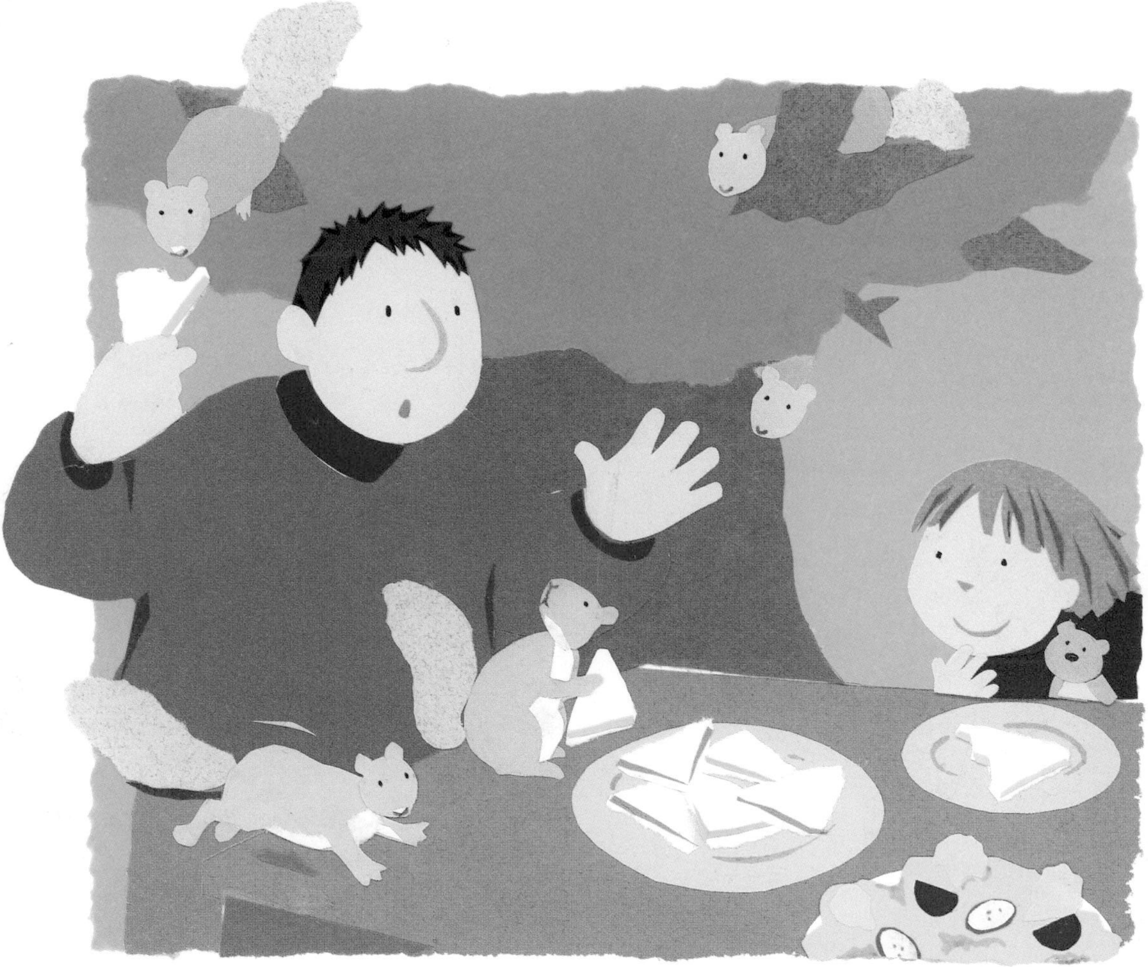

the squirrels